This Book is For:

_____

With Lots of Love
From:

_____

On This Date:

_____

This one's for you, kid.
—B.H.

For EE. Thanks for the hugs. X
—D.E.

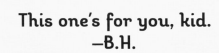

ZONDERKIDZ

You're the Hugs to My Kisses
Copyright © 2022 by Barbara Herndon
Illustrations © 2022 by Diane Ewen

Requests for information should be addressed to:

Zonderkidz, 3900 *Sparks Drive SE, Grand Rapids, Michigan* 49546

Hardcover ISBN 978-0-310-73496-3
Ebook ISBN 978-0-310-xxxxx-x

Art Direction & Design: Jody Langley

Printed in Malaysia

22 23 24 25 26 27 28 /IMG/ 15 14 13 12 11 10 9 8 7 6 5 4 3 2 1

You're the Hugs to my Kisses

Celebrating Family & Friendship

written by
Barbara Herndon

illustrated by
Diane Ewen

You're the jelly to my donut.

You're the blue to my sky.

You're the laces to my sneakers.

You're the twinkle to my eye.

You're the milk to my cookies.

You're the smile to my face.

You're the ketchup to my French fries.

You're the flower to my vase.

You're the icing to my cupcake.

You're the sunshine to my day.

You're the water to my ocean.

You're the laughter
to my play.

You're the upside to my down.

You're the hero to my story.

You're the jewel to my crown.

You're the bubbles to my bathtub.

You're the bouncy
to my bed.

You're the hugs to my kisses.

You're the pillow to my head.

You're the sweet dreams to my slumber.

You're the answer to my prayer.

And whether you are near or far ...

We are the perfect pair.